1989

Monsters in the Outfield

Young Yearling books you will enjoy:

The Pee Wee Scouts books by Judy Delton

Cookies and Crutches
Camp Ghost-Away
Lucky Dog Days
Blue Skies, French Fries

The Polka Dot Private Eye books by Patricia Reilly Giff

The Mystery of the Blue Ring
The Riddle of the Red Purse
The Secret at the Polk Street School
The Powder Puff Puzzle

Yearling Books/Young Yearlings/Yearling Classics are designed especially to entertain and enlighten young people. Patricia Reilly Giff, consultant to this series, received the bachelor's degree from Marymount College. She holds the master's degree in history from St. John's University and a Professional Diploma in Reading from Hofstra University. She was a teacher and reading consultant for many years and is the author of numerous books for young readers.

For a complete listing of all Yearling titles, write to:
Dell Readers Service, P.O. Box 1045,
South Holland, IL 60473.

Monsters in the Outfield

--- ♦ ---

Stephen Mooser

Illustrated by George Ulrich

A YOUNG YEARLING BOOK

Published by
Dell Publishing
a division of
Bantam Doubleday Dell Publishing Group, Inc.
666 Fifth Avenue
New York, New York 10103

The trademark Yearling ® is registered in the U.S. Patent and
Trademark Office.

ISBN: 0-440-40219-0

Printed in the United States of America

October 1989

10 9 8 7 6 5 4 3 2 1

W

For Jennie and Rose Dobbs

Contents

Chapter 1

◆

Henry Potter

Henry Potter was a big bragger.

"I am the greatest," he said one day at school.

His friend Rosa Dorado laughed. "You're the greatest bigmouth in the world."

Henry and Rosa were standing in line to play handball. As usual, Henry's hair was sticking up in back. Like a feather.

"Handball is easy," said Henry. "I can beat anybody."

"You couldn't beat a flea," said Rosa. She loved to tease Henry. "Wait till we play. I'll kill you."

Just then Henry saw Zack Morton coming their way. Zack's head was down. His fists were clenched. And he was kicking up dirt.

"Oh-oh," whispered Henry. "Here comes trouble."

"He better not start anything," said Rosa.

Zack was captain of the Sharks. The Sharks called themselves a baseball team. But most of them were just bullies. Zack was the worst of all.

He walked right to the front of the line.

"I'm cutting in," he said. He pushed aside a first grader. "It's my turn."

"Hey, big ears!" said Henry. Zack did have big ears. But then, he also had big arms. And a big head with a flat top. Most people were scared of Zack. But not Henry. Besides, he wanted to show off for Rosa.

Henry said, "Get in the back of the line."

Zack did as he was told. He stomped to the back of the line.

"Potter, I got something for you," he said. He made a fist and growled.

Then, *pow!* Zack hit Henry.

Now Henry had a big lip to go along with his big mouth.

Henry watched Zack walk away. He tried hard not to cry.

"Someday I'll get even," he said. He made a fist. "Someday that bully and I will meet again. Then, *pow!* He'll be the sorry one."

Chapter 2

◆

The Big Bite

Henry didn't go home after school. Instead he walked to Rosa's house. He went there almost every day. So did all the members of the Creepy Creature Club. Everyone in the club loved monsters. They collected monster trading cards. They went to scary movies together. And this month they were going to put on a play in Rosa's garage. The play was called *Return of the Vampire*. They were going to charge a quarter to get in. They hoped to make enough money to fix up Rosa's garage. They wanted to make it into a haunted house. It was going to be the scariest place in town.

Henry liked something else about the

Dorado house. That something was Rosa. Henry thought she was the prettiest girl in the world. Someday he was going to tell her that he liked her. Someday. Soon.

On the way to Rosa's, Henry picked a flower. It was a big red rose.

"I'll give this to Rosa," he said. "Then she will know that I like her."

When Henry got to Rosa's he smoothed down his hair so his feather wouldn't stick up. Then he put the rose behind his back and knocked.

"Eyeball soup," he said, giving the secret password.

Rosa opened the garage door.

"Henry!" she gasped. "Your lip. It looks terrible."

Henry couldn't reply. He was too busy wondering what had happened to Rosa. She looked terrible. Her black hair was in tangles. There was blood on her cheek. And there was a big cut on her neck.

"Rosa! Are you all right?"

Rosa laughed. So did all the other Creepy Creature Club members. They were sitting on a long green couch. Behind the couch

one whole wall was covered with monster posters. Nearby, a pile of scary masks laid on a table. Hanging above all this, twisting slowly, was a giant rubber spider.

"Rosa, how did you get cut?" asked Henry.

"I didn't get cut," said Rosa. Her voice was shaking. "I got bit!"

Henry gulped. He looked around.

"Rosa was bitten by Dracula," said red-haired Ginger Stein. She lowered her voice. "Be careful. The vampire is still in the room."

Henry gulped twice. Then he remembered something. Today was the day they were going to try on the makeup for the play. The monster makeup.

Henry studied Rosa's neck. He saw that it was just a fake scar. The blood was only catsup.

"Hey! Wait a minute," he said. "I thought I was the club's makeup artist." He was starting to get angry. "Who took my job?"

"Mort Burns did," said Rosa. She stuck her sharp nose in the air. "Admit it, Henry Potter. There is someone in the world better than you."

Henry scratched his head. "Who is Mort Burns?"

Rosa held up a fat book. It was called *Secrets of Monster Makeup*. There was a picture of a monster on the cover. He had bulging eyes and a face full of slimy warts.

"Yuck!" said Henry. "Is that Mort Burns?"

"No, silly," said Rosa. "Mort Burns wrote the book. He taught me how to make the scar."

"That scar does look real," said Henry. "Still, I could have done a better job."

Everyone laughed. Everyone but Melvin Purdy. Melvin was the littlest member of the club. He was scrunched down in a corner of the couch like a wadded-up sweater. In his arms he had a tiny gray dog. The dog's name was Flip. He was the Creature Club mascot.

"Can't we do another play?" asked Melvin. He had a voice like a mouse. Supersoft. "Please, monsters scare me."

Henry rolled his eyes. Everything scared Melvin Purdy. Even merry-go-round horses.

"Why don't we do *Peter Rabbit*?" squeaked Melvin. "That's a nice story."

8

Rosa went over and put a hand on Melvin's shoulder. "If you are so afraid of monsters, why are you in our club?"

Melvin hugged the dog. "If I wasn't in the club I couldn't play with Flip. Flip is my best friend."

Flip licked Melvin on the face. Then he jumped off Melvin's lap, barked, and turned a flip in the air. Flip liked Melvin too. They were never apart.

Suddenly, Henry remembered the flower.

"Surprise!" said Henry. He put the flower in Rosa's face. "A rose for a Rosa."

Rosa gasped and quickly pushed away the flower. *"Ah . . . ah . . . ah—"* she said.

"No, it's okay," said Henry. He put the flower under her nose again. "I want you to have it."

"But I . . . *ah . . . ah . . . ah . . .*" said Rosa, stepping back. "Henry, I . . . *ah . . . ah . . . ah—*"

"Don't be shy," said Henry. "Go on. Take it." He tickled her nose with the rose. "Doesn't it smell nice?"

"Ah . . . ah . . . choo!" sneezed Rosa.

She sniffled. "Henry Potter! Sometimes you're so dumb!"

"Dumb? For giving you a flower?" Henry was very confused.

Rosa took out a handkerchief. She blew her nose. "Flowers make me sneeze," she said. "Didn't you—*ah choo!*—know that?"

"No, I ..." For once Henry didn't have anything to say. He felt terrible. Everyone was looking.

Rosa blew her nose again. "I've got an allergy," she said. "I have to be careful around lots of—*ah choo!*—things."

Rosa twisted the handkerchief in her hands. She looked embarrassed.

Henry felt embarrassed too.

"I'm sorry," he said. "I'll never give you a flower again. I promise."

"I hope not," said Rosa. She gave Henry a long, hard look. It was not the kind of look that said "I like you."

Henry sighed. And Rosa clapped her hands.

"All right," she said. "Let's start the—*ah choo!*—meeting."

The meeting lasted an hour. Everyone was given a job.

Melvin would help with the costumes. Ginger would paint the scenery. Henry would help Rosa with the makeup. The others would make signs and put them up in town. Everybody would act in the play.

"The play will be in ten days," said Rosa. "On Saturday. At three—*ah choo!*—o'clock."

Rosa blew her nose. "Henry Potter, you and your stupid—*ah choo!*—flower!"

For the tenth time, Henry said, "I'm sorry."

And for the hundredth time, Rosa answered, *"Ah choo!"*

Chapter 3

♦

Ingredients

On Monday Henry's class took a spelling test.

"Everyone take out some paper," said the teacher, Ms. Hatfield.

Rosa leaned across the aisle. She tapped Henry on the arm.

"Henry, ingredients," she said.

Henry looked straight ahead.

"Ingredients!" repeated Rosa.

"I know I'm the best speller in class," said Henry. "But I'm sorry. If I helped you it would be cheating. Spell 'ingredients' yourself. Just sound it out."

Suddenly, a note landed on Henry's desk. He opened it up. It was a list of things to get. Catsup was on the list. So were cotton and eggs.

He looked at Rosa. "What's this?"

"Ingredients. For the makeup. Bring them to my house on Friday. We can work on the makeup then."

Henry blushed. "I thought you wanted help with your spelling."

"From you?" said Rosa. She laughed. "Henry Potter, everyone knows you can't spell worth beans."

Henry looked at the note and smiled. It was the first note he'd ever gotten from Rosa. He guessed that it meant she liked him.

All day long Henry read Rosa's note over and over.

"Henry," it began. "Bring these things to my house on Friday: cotton, food coloring, catsup, eggs, and rubber cement."

Henry liked the ending best of all. It said: "Thank you, Rosa."

"What a nice way to end a letter," thought Henry. "I guess Rosa must really like me."

After school Henry headed for home. On the way he saw Melvin Purdy sitting on a bus bench. Melvin didn't see Henry coming. He was reading a magazine, *Baseball Superstars.*

"Hey, Melvin!" shouted Henry. He slapped his friend on the back. "What's up?"

Melvin jumped a foot. "Yikes!" he shouted. The magazine flew into the air.

"Melvin. It's only me. Henry."

Melvin drew in a deep breath. He put his hand on his heart.

"He- ... He- ... Henry," he said. "You scared me half to death."

"I only wanted to say hello," said Henry.

"Well, d- ... d- ... don't do it again," said Melvin. He sighed. "Please."

Henry bent down and picked up the magazine. A picture of a baseball player was on the cover. Above the picture it said: "Meet Matt Jackson. He's the Best Hitter in Baseball."

"When I grow up I'll be even better than Matt Jackson," bragged Henry. "Then my picture will be on the cover."

Henry returned the magazine to Melvin. Then he took out Rosa's note.

"Did you know that Rosa likes me?" said Henry. "She sends me notes all the time."

"Really?" said Melvin.

"Sure," said Henry. He crossed his fingers. "That's how close we are."

15

Melvin was jealous. He liked Rosa too. But he was afraid to admit it. He bit his lip. "Does she really send you notes?"

"Sure," said Henry. "Just look at this."

Henry handed Melvin the note. Melvin read off the words. Then he squinted. And read them again.

"This is just a shopping list," said Melvin. He handed it back. "I get notes like this all the time. From my mom."

Henry shook his head. Poor Melvin, he thought. He doesn't know anything. Didn't he read the ending? The part that said "thank you." Would Rosa have written that if she didn't like him?

Henry folded the note carefully. Then he put it in his pocket. "When someone likes you they send you a note," said Henry.

"That isn't what my best friend does," said Melvin.

"Oh, what does he do," asked Henry, "phone you?"

"Nope," said Melvin. "He wags his tail!"

Chapter 4

◆

Bigmouth Strikes Again

The next day Henry got behind Zack in the cafeteria line.

"Say, Zack," he began. "Ever hear of a baseball player named Matt Jackson?"

Zack looked down at Henry. "Yeah, I heard of him," he growled.

"He's the greatest hitter in baseball. He's a real superstar," said Henry.

"He is a good hitter," said Zack. "Hey! Where did you learn so much about baseball?"

"I know everything about baseball," said Henry. He puffed out his chest. "I'm a real expert."

They came to the end of the line. Zack

scraped his peas into the garbage can. "Potter, I bet you don't know a baseball from a basement."

"Oh, yeah?" said Henry. He scraped off his peas too. "Baseball is my middle name. I'm the greatest player ever. Someday you'll see me on the cover of *Baseball Superstars*."

"Don't make me laugh," said Zack.

The cafeteria grew quiet. Everyone looked at Henry and Zack. They were standing toe to toe. Tray to tray. It looked like there might be another fight.

Zack said, "You're not a baseball player. You're just a bigmouth."

Henry banged his tray down on a table. His hot dog jumped a foot. "Are you calling me a liar?"

"I'm saying you can't play baseball," said Zack.

"All right then," said Henry. He was trying to act calm, but his face was tomato red. "We'll see who's best. I challenge you to a game. The Creepy Creature Club against the Sharks."

"That would be a real laugh," said Zack.

"Only because we'd win," said Henry. "I'd bet anything we'd stomp you."

Zack raised an eyebrow. "You'd bet anything?"

"Sure," said Henry, without thinking.

"Okay then," said Zack. "Let's bet. If you win, the Sharks promise to help fix up your clubhouse."

"And what if you win?" asked Henry.

"Then you have to give us that little dog. The one that turns those flips," said Zack. "He'd make a great mascot for the Sharks."

Henry gulped. "I don't know. Flip means a lot to our club."

"What's wrong? Chicken?" said Zack. He poked Henry in the chest. "I thought you said you'd stomp us."

Henry bit his lip. Everyone in the cafeteria was looking.

He took a deep breath. "All right," he said. He shook Zack's hand. "It's a deal."

"The game will be next Saturday. At noon. In Bluebird Park," said Zack. He poked Henry again. "Don't chicken out."

"Don't worry," said Henry. He gave Zack a long, hard look. "Just don't *you* chicken out."

Zack snorted and walked over to the Sharks' table. He sat down and whispered something to his friend Angie Dobbs. Then they both looked at Henry. And started to laugh.

The cafeteria was buzzing. Everyone was talking about the same thing. The big game.

Billy Mays, a third grader, said to his friend Bob, "I hope Henry's team beats those bullies."

"Me too," said Bob. "But let's face it. They don't have a chance. That Creepy Creature Club is going to get creamed."

Chapter 5

◆

In Trouble

As it turned out, Henry almost did get creamed. That very afternoon. By his own friends.

"Henry Potter!" screamed Rosa the moment he walked into the garage. "What's wrong with you? Did someone kidnap your brain?"

Henry took a step back. "Hey, wait a—"

"Why did you say we'd play the Sharks?" said Rosa, waving her arms. "Potato brain! We don't even have a team!"

Henry gulped. Potato brain! Did this mean Rosa didn't like him anymore?

"You and your big mouth," she continued. She shook a finger in Henry's face. "Tomorrow, tell Zack that the game is off."

"We can't back out," said Henry. "Everyone in school saw me make the bet. I shook on it." He looked around the room. "Do you want everyone to think we're chickens?"

Melvin Purdy was sitting on the couch, hugging Flip. "Did you really tell Zack he could have our dog?" he whispered.

"Well ... I ..." mumbled Henry.

Melvin looked ready to cry. "Henry, did you?" He began to sniffle.

Henry sighed. "Yes. It's true. I did. But don't worry, we won't lose."

Big tears ran down Melvin's cheeks. "It's not fair. It's not. Flip is my best friend."

Henry held out his hands. "Hey! What's the big worry? We'll kill those Sharks. I bet anything we will."

"You and your stupid bets," said Rosa. She put her hands on her hips. "How could you do this to us?"

"But, Rosa," said Henry. "I was only—"

"Another thing," said Ginger, interrupting. "The game is on Saturday. So is the play." She waved a piece of paper in his face. "Look. The posters about the play are already made. We're putting them up tomorrow."

Henry took the poster from Ginger. He read it carefully. Then he said, "What's the big deal? The game is at noon. The play isn't until three. We can do both."

"Forget it," said Rosa. She lifted up her nose and turned her back on Henry. "We're actors, not baseball players."

"We have to at least try," said Henry. He made a fist. "Come on. Do you want to lose Flip?"

"We'd better not lose Flip," said Rosa. She spun around and pointed her finger at Henry. "If we do I'll never talk to you again."

Henry gulped.

"And I'll never talk to you again either," said Melvin. He hugged Flip. "Maybe I'll never talk to anyone again."

"Listen," said Henry, "we can practice tomorrow after we put up the posters. Maybe we're better than we think."

"Maybe we're worse," said Rosa. She put her hands on her hips. "Henry Potter, you

and your big mouth have just wrecked our club."

"Wrecked the club!" said Henry. "Wait a minute. If we win, the Sharks have to fix up the clubhouse. Gee, I thought I was doing us a favor."

"Some favor," said Rosa.

"Some friend," said Melvin.

"Some mistake," thought Henry. "Why can't I learn to keep my big trap shut?"

Chapter 6

◆

Practice, Sort of

After school on Wednesday the Creepy Creature Club put up signs all over town. Soon every telephone pole had a sign that read:

The Creepy Creature Club Presents ...

Return of the Vampire

Thrills! Chills! Monsters Galore!

3 P.M. Saturday
1265 River Street

*   *   *   25 ¢   *   *   *

Be There If You Dare!

27

After the town had been papered, the club met at Bluebird Park for baseball practice. It was a big park, mostly grass. At one end there were swings, a slide, and monkey bars. At the other end was the baseball diamond. A screen was at the back of the diamond, and on the sides were some benches.

The Creepy Creature Club walked across the park. Flip led the way, running and yelping and turning flips.

Henry was just behind Flip. He had a mitt in one hand and a ball in the other. In his pocket he had a candy bar. He had bought it for Rosa.

"Sweets for the sweet," he told himself. "When the time is right I'm going to give it to her. Then she'll know I like her."

"Oh-oh, trouble," said Melvin. "Look. It's the Sharks. They're sitting on the benches."

"They can't stop us from practicing," said Rosa. She had a bat in her hand. "This park is for everyone."

"Well, look who's coming," shouted Zack. He poked Angie Dobbs in the ribs. "It's that silly monster club."

Angie had long, stringy hair. It hung down her back like a dirty brown waterfall. "Oh, look," she said. "They brought that cute dog. The one that's going to be our new mascot."

Zack stood up. He had a scrunched-up nose and a ton of freckles. "Come here, dog," he said, waving at Flip. "Come over and do some tricks."

Flip stopped and looked at Zack. He tilted his head and perked up his ears.

"I said get over here!" yelled Zack. "What's wrong with that mutt? Is he stupid or something?"

Melvin Purdy ran up and put his arms around Flip. "Leave my dog alone," he said softly. "He's mine."

"Only till Saturday," said Zack. "Then he's ours." Zack shook a finger at Flip. "Doggie, you'll learn to obey me then. Or else."

Rosa took the ball from Henry. She walked over to home plate. "Come on, everybody. Let's practice catching. I'll hit you some balls. Don't pay attention to the Sharks."

The Creepy Creature Club took the field.

Henry went to first base. Ginger went to second. And Melvin went to third. Everyone else—Curly, Darlene, Jody, and the others—ran to the outfield.

"Get ready!" cried Rosa. She threw the ball up into the air and hit it to Ginger. "Here it comes! Catch it!"

Swoosh! The ball went right through Ginger's legs.

"Nice catch!" laughed one of the Sharks.

Ginger lowered her eyes.

"Don't listen to them," said Rosa. "You'll catch it next time."

"Only if she uses a net!" shouted Zack. The other Sharks howled at his joke.

Next Rosa hit a high fly ball to Henry.

"I got it! I got it!" cried Henry, backing up.

Henry had his eyes on the ball. But his mind was on Rosa. He wanted to show off.

"I'm going to catch this one-handed," he said to himself.

Suddenly, Henry slipped. *Plop!* He dropped right onto the seat of his pants. The ball landed two feet away, in the dirt.

"Nice catch!" yelled Zack.

"Butterfingers!" shouted the other Sharks.

Henry got to his feet. "Shut your traps," he muttered. He bent over and dusted himself off.

"We'll shut our traps when you shut your pants," said Zack.

"Huh?" said Henry. He couldn't figure out why all the Sharks were suddenly pointing at him and laughing.

"Henry!" cried Rosa. "Your pants!"

Henry patted the back of his pants. They were torn. He could feel his skin through the hole.

"Oooooeeeee!" said Zack.

All the Sharks began whistling.

"Oooooeeeee!"

Henry put one hand over the hole. Then he pointed the other one at the Sharks.

"Get lost!" he yelled. "Bug off."

To everyone's surprise, that was just what they did. One by one they got up from the bench. Then, laughing and pointing, they strolled out of the park.

"Those Sharks are lucky I didn't beat them up," said Henry. "Everyone knows

I'm the best fighter in school. The toughest too. They'll be sorry. Next time."

At last the Creepy Creatures could practice in peace.

But even in peace the practice was a disaster.

Almost.

There was one bright spot. Ginger turned out to be a good pitcher.

She pitched to everyone. Everybody struck out. Except for Rosa. She got a hit.

Whack! The ball went right at the third baseman, Melvin.

"Yikes!" yelled Melvin.

"Catch it!" cried Henry.

But Melvin was too scared to make the catch. He acted as if the ball coming his way were a pack of rats. Starving ones.

"Yikes!" he said again, jumping out of the way. The ball rolled into the outfield. Rosa ran to first.

Ginger shook her head. "It's hopeless," she cried. "Our team is horrible. We're going to lose the game, and our dog."

"Maybe Zack will take back the bet," said Rosa.

"I don't think so," said Henry. "When was the last time you saw Zack Morton do something nice?"

"We have to at least ask," said Rosa. She looked out into the field. Flip was chasing a butterfly. "I couldn't stand to see the Sharks get our little puppy."

Henry looked into Rosa's big brown eyes. He had never seen her look so pretty. He wanted to tell her she was beautiful. But he was afraid.

Just then he remembered the candy bar. He took it out of his pocket. It was mushy. But he held it out anyway.

Shuffling his feet, he said, "Rosa, I got something for you. I bought it myself."

Rosa looked at the candy bar. Her lip curled back. "Candy! What is this, Henry? A joke?"

"No. It's sweets for the sweet," muttered Henry, embarrassed.

"Please, don't tease me," said Rosa. "Didn't you know? I can't eat sugar."

Henry's heart sank. "Can't eat sugar! How come? Does it make you sneeze?"

"No, of course not," said Rosa. "It's bad

for my teeth." She shook a finger at Henry. "You shouldn't eat candy either. Do you want to get cavities?"

Henry's mouth felt dry. "No ... I just. .." He sighed. "I'm sorry. I just wanted to do something nice for you."

Rosa watched Henry put the candy back in his pocket. "Look," she said, "if you want to do something nice, talk to Zack. Call off the bet."

Henry smiled. "All right. I'll do it. Just for you. I'll talk to Zack tomorrow."

"Why wait till tomorrow?" asked Rosa. She pointed toward the street. "Here come the Sharks."

Everyone looked up. Sure enough, Zack and the Sharks came running through the gate. All nine of them.

They were laughing and running. And throwing paper airplanes.

Chapter 7

◆

Litterbugs

A paper airplane landed at Rosa's feet. She bent down and picked it up.

"Oh no!" she gasped.

"What's wrong?" asked Ginger.

Rosa unfolded the plane.

"Look," she said. "It's our sign. One that we just put up."

Henry looked over Rosa's shoulder. He read off the words: "The Creepy Creature Club Presents ..."

Now planes were coming down everywhere. Like giant snowflakes. And each one was the same. A club poster.

Henry was boiling mad. He snatched up a plane.

"What is this?" he shouted, waving it at Zack.

Zack grinned. "Looks to me like an airplane."

He turned and winked at the Sharks. "But then, it could be just trash."

The Sharks laughed. And slapped their knees.

Rosa clenched her teeth. She had worked hard to make the signs, even harder to put them up.

"Zack Morton, you'll pay for this," she said. "You ruined our signs."

"We'll go to the police," said Henry. "I have lots of friends there."

The Sharks laughed. Angie Dobbs said, "We're the ones that should go to the police. You're the litterbugs, not us."

"Litterbugs?" said Henry.

"Yeah. You littered every pole in town," said Angie. "Thanks to us the town is clean again."

"Maybe the mayor will give us a medal," said Zack.

Henry thought they should get medals too—dropped onto their heads. From the Empire State Building.

Ginger took out a handkerchief. She blew

her nose. "Now no one will come to the play."

Rosa folded her arms across her chest. "Don't worry, Ginger. We'll put them back up."

"Don't waste your time," said Zack. "You put them up, we'll take them down."

"We want a clean town," said Angie.

"Besides," said Zack, "how can you be in a play on Saturday? Remember, the game is that day."

Henry sighed. He had to ask Zack to take back his bet.

"About the game ..." began Henry.

"Yeah," snarled Zack. "What about it?"

Henry sighed again. This was the hardest thing he had ever had to do. He looked down at Flip. The little dog was wagging his tail.

"Zack, the gang and I were wondering if we could forget the bet. Can we call off the game?"

"No way!" said Angie. "I want that dog."

"A bet is a bet," said Zack. "The whole school saw you make it."

"But ..." said Henry.

"No buts," said Zack. "Play on Saturday, or give us the mutt now."

"No," said Melvin. "Please, no." He picked up Flip and held him close.

Henry looked at his friends. They were staring at the ground. "The Sharks are all talk," he said. "We can beat them. Easy."

"We've got to beat them," said Melvin. He hugged Flip. "We've just got to. Flip means everything to me."

Rosa poked Henry in the chest. "This is all your fault! Pea brain!"

Henry looked into Rosa's big brown eyes. She was mad. Real mad.

"I'm sorry," he said. "Boy, you make me feel like the biggest rat in the world."

"If I were you," said Rosa, "I wouldn't brag about it."

Chapter 8

◆

Baseball Practice

The Creepy Creature Club practiced baseball for two more days. But they didn't get any better. Ginger was a good pitcher. Everyone else was terrible.

The grass in the field made Rosa sneeze. Henry couldn't hit.

And Melvin was scared of the ball.

"Yikes!" he would yell whenever the ball came his way. Then he would run.

"It's hopeless," said Rosa. "The Creepy Creature Club is the worst team ever. We're going to lose, for—*ah choo!*—sure."

Chapter 9

◆

The Ugliest Girl in the World

On Friday, the day before the game, Henry went to Rosa's garage. He brought all the makeup ingredients in a big brown bag.

"Eyeball soup," he said, knocking.

Henry patted down his hair.

"This is it," he said to himself. "Today I'm going to tell Rosa I like her. I'm going to tell her she's the most beautiful girl in the world."

Rosa opened the door.

"Hi," said Henry, smiling.

"Oh," said Rosa, "it's you."

Henry held up the bag. "I brought the ingredients. You know, the makeup for our play."

Rosa sighed. "I guess we better get started." She narrowed her eyes. "After all, tomorrow is a busy day. We have to be in a baseball game *and* a play, thanks to you!"

Henry tried to keep smiling. "Where shall I put the bag?"

"On the table," said Rosa, pointing. "I'll get the monster makeup book."

Henry set out the ingredients. Soon Rosa was back with the book, a bowl, and a spoon.

"First let's make a scar," said Rosa. "Hand me the rubber cement."

Henry gave her the jar.

"Now give me the red food coloring," she said.

Henry gave her the food coloring.

Rosa went to work. She poured out a blob of rubber cement. Then she dropped in some food coloring.

"When this dries we will have an ugly scar," said Rosa.

Henry didn't hear a word she said. He

had his elbows on the table. And his chin in his hands. He couldn't stop staring at Rosa. "She's so pretty," he thought.

Rosa kept working. Henry kept dreaming. And thinking.

"Very soon I am going to tell Rosa she is pretty," he thought. "Today I won't give her flowers. Or candy. Only words. Soon. I'll tell her I like her."

But he couldn't. Not just then. He was too nervous.

"Now we must make some green slime for me," said Rosa. "Remember, I'll be a zombie in the play."

"You will be a beautiful zombie," thought Henry. "The prettiest zombie ever."

Rosa began mixing things in the bowl. She put in two raw eggs. She added some green coloring. Then she mixed up the slimy goo with a wooden spoon.

Rosa let the slime drip from the spoon.

"This sure looks yucky," she said.

"You sure look pretty," thought Henry. But he was afraid to say it out loud.

Rosa dabbed some slime onto her face.

"I'm going to get ugly," she said.

44

"You could never be ugly, sweet Rosa," thought Henry.

Soon Rosa's face was covered with slime. She looked horrible. Really dreadful.

She turned to Henry. "How do I look?" she asked.

Henry swallowed. This was his big chance. "Rosa," he said, "you look pretty."

"What!" she said.

"You are the prettiest girl in the world," he said.

"Henry Potter, what a horrible thing to say! I worked hard to look ugly. Very hard."

"I'm sorry," said Henry. "What I meant was . . ."

Just then there was a knock at the door. It was Melvin Purdy. He stuck his head in.

"Can I come in?" he asked. "I'm looking for Flip."

"Flip is in the back," said Rosa.

"Thank you," said Melvin. He looked up. Suddenly, he saw Rosa for the first time.

"Yikes!" he screamed. His hair nearly stood on end. "Yikes. A monster!"

"Melvin, it's only Rosa!" shouted Henry.

46

"Calm down." Henry rolled his eyes. "Boy," he thought. "What a baby."

Melvin couldn't stop shaking. He stared long and hard at Rosa. "Rosa, you're the ugliest person I've ever seen."

Rosa beamed. "Why thank you, Melvin." She gave Henry a dirty look. "See. Melvin likes my makeup."

"But ... but I do too," said Henry. "I think you're a great zombie. The ugliest!"

"You're just saying that," said Rosa.

"No, no, I really mean it," said Henry. "Rosa, you are very, very ugly."

"I'm sorry. I don't believe you," said Rosa. She walked over to Melvin and put a hand on his shoulder. "Come along, Melvin. Let's find Flip."

Henry watched them walk out the door.

"Rosa!" he yelled. "You've got to believe me. Rosa, you're ugly! Very, very ugly! Rosa!"

Chapter 10

♦

The Monster All-Stars

At last the big day arrived.

Henry had breakfast, then he hurried to Rosa's.

A mummy greeted him at the door. It was Ginger. She was wrapped in strips of cloth from head to toe.

"Why are you in costume?" asked Henry. "The game comes first. Then the play."

"There won't be time to change," said Ginger. "We're going to play the game in our costumes."

"That's right," said Rosa. She was holding the bowl of green slime in her hands. "We're going to be the Monster All-Stars. After the game we'll hurry back and put on the play."

"The Monster All-Stars," said Henry. "I like that name."

"It's a perfect name, for a horrible team," said Ginger.

Rosa set the bowl on the table. Next to the bowl were some scars, some sharp teeth, and four lumpy warts. Rosa stuck a wooden spoon into the green slime. She stirred up the goo. Then she lifted out the dripping spoon.

"Makeup time," she yelled. "Come and get it!"

Everyone lined up. Then Henry helped her do terrible things to all their friends.

They put an ugly scar on Curly.

They gave Darlene sharp teeth. And a hairy face.

They put giant warts on the nose of a creature from Mars—Melvin.

Finally, Henry put in his vampire fangs. And Rosa covered her face with slime.

"Ugh, a zombie," said Ginger. "Rosa, you look horrible."

"Not as horrible as me," said Henry. He smiled, showing off his pointed teeth. "Admit it. I am the worst of all."

Rosa thought about Henry's big mouth. And about how they might soon lose Flip.

"We admit it," said Rosa. "Everyone agrees. You're the worst."

Henry smiled. "Why, thank you. What a nice thing to say."

Then it was time to go to the game.

The Creepy Creature Club marched out of the clubhouse. In a single file they headed for Bluebird Park. Flip followed along behind, barking and yelping and turning flips.

Ms. Harper was working in her garden when the Monsters went by.

"Oh, my," she said, pushing back her hat. "Is it Halloween?"

Mr. Porter was at his mailbox when he saw them coming.

"Is someone making a monster movie?" he wondered aloud.

"Nope," said Henry. "We're a baseball team."

"Huh?" said Mr. Porter. He scratched his head. He'd never seen anything like the Monster All-Stars.

At last they came to Bluebird Park. It looked like the whole school was there—

50

maybe the whole town. Everyone was near the baseball diamond. Some people had brought chairs. Others were sitting on the grass.

The Sharks were already on the field. Zack was standing at home plate batting balls to his team. They looked good. They had on white uniforms with blue sharks on the back. And they never missed a catch. Or a throw.

Henry yelled, "Gangway for the Monster All-Stars!"

The monsters ran through the gate. Into the park they charged.

The crowd gasped.

"Mo- ... mo- ... monsters!" screamed a little boy.

"Help!" screeched his baby sister.

The Wilson twins (they were only three) started to run.

The Monster All-Stars dashed onto the field.

The Sharks stopped what they were doing. For a moment they looked scared. Not one of them moved. Finally Zack said, "What's going on?"

Henry the vampire walked over. He showed

Zack his sharp teeth. He took a long look at Zack's neck, as if he wanted to bite it.

Zack gulped. Squinting, he leaned in close. "Henry Potter? Is that you?"

"Yep," said Henry. "The Monster All-Stars are here. Let's play."

"I never played a vampire before," said Zack. He looked over at Ginger. "Or a mummy."

"Do you want to call off the game?" asked Henry. "Too scared to play?"

Melvin was standing next to Henry. He crossed his fingers. He was hoping Zack would be too scared to play.

"Don't make me laugh," said Zack. "Sharks aren't afraid of anything." He turned suddenly and looked right at Melvin. "Boo!" he shouted.

Melvin jumped a foot. The antennas on his head wagged wildly, like a pair of puppy dog's tails.

Zack laughed. "It looks to me like it's the Monsters who are scared."

Henry put his arm on Melvin's shoulder.

"Shut up, Zack," he said. "We're not afraid of you. Are we, Melvin?"

"No," whispered Melvin. But he didn't look as if he meant it. Not the way he was shaking. Like jelly. In an earthquake.

53

Chapter 11

♦

The Vampire behind Home Plate

The game began.

The Monsters took the field. Henry was the catcher. Ginger was the pitcher. And Rosa played second base.

"*Ah choo!*" went Rosa the moment she got on the field. "The grass is making me sneeze. It's my allergy."

"Don't worry about it," yelled Henry. "It will go away."

But it didn't. Every few minutes the second baseman went "*Ah choo!*"

The first batter was Angie Dobbs.

Just before Ginger pitched the ball, Henry whispered to Angie, "What a nice neck you have. A skinny neck. The kind a vampire likes."

"Huh?" said Angie, turning around.

Just then Ginger's pitch came whizzing by.

"Strike one!" cried the umpire.

"I'm hungry," growled Henry. "Got any blood for me, Angie?"

Angie lowered her bat. She rubbed her neck.

Ginger threw again.

"Strike two!" yelled the umpire.

Henry smacked his lips together. "This vampire wants to eat!"

Angie was afraid to turn her back. She couldn't take her eyes off Henry's sharp teeth.

"Strike three! You're out!" said the umpire as the ball zipped past again.

Angie hurried away.

Henry laughed. He stood up and faced the Sharks. Hissing, he showed them his teeth.

"Next victim, please," he said.

At first, no Sharks wanted to bat. Finally Zack pushed a skinny little Shark up to the plate.

"Your neck looks tasty," said Henry to the poor, shaking boy. "Have any blood for me today?"

Like Angie, the boy couldn't take his eyes off Henry's fangs. And, like Angie, he struck out. On three straight pitches.

After the next Shark had struck out, too, Zack ran up to Henry.

"You're not playing fair," he said. "You're scaring us."

Henry didn't answer. All he did was show his teeth. Then he started to laugh. A deep, scary vampire's laugh. Zack shivered. Then he turned and hurried away.

Now it was the Monsters' turn to bat.

Ginger the mummy was up first.

"Get a hit!" yelled Henry.

And she did! The ball went right past third base.

"Run!" yelled Henry.

Ginger turned past first and headed for second. But just then her costume began to unwrap. The cloth spun off her body

57

like paper towels off a roll. Halfway to second she tripped on the cloth and fell.

Angie Dobbs ran over and tagged her out. Hard. On the head.

"Ouch!" said Ginger. "That hurt."

"Oh," said Angie, "does the mummy want her mummy?"

Ginger didn't answer. She bit her lip. Then she walked away, trailing her costume behind her.

Chapter 12

◆

The Big Play

The Monsters couldn't score. Luckily, the Sharks couldn't either. Ginger kept striking them out. With the help of a vampire catcher, of course.

Then, in the fourth inning, the Sharks got a run.

It all started with Angie Dobbs. She hit the first pitch on the ground to Melvin.

"Yikes!" he screamed. "The ball! It's coming my way!"

Without thinking, he took off like a rabbit. A scared one.

The ball rolled into the outfield. And Angie ended up on second base.

Next up was Zack Morton.

"Strike him out!" yelled the crowd. They wanted the Monsters to beat the bullies.

But Zack didn't strike out. Instead he hit a high fly ball to Rosa. "I got it!" she yelled. "I . . . *ah . . . ah . . . ah . . .*"

A sneeze was coming on. She tried to stop it. *"Ah . . . ah . . . ah . . ."* But then, just before the ball got to her glove, she went, *"choo!"*

The ball bounced off her glove and rolled away. Angie scored, and the Sharks took the lead. One to nothing.

"Ah choo!" said Zack, laughing. "Thanks for the help, Sneezy!"

"Stop making fun!" yelled Henry. "She's got an allergy."

"Isn't that too bad," said Zack. "I think I'm going to cry."

Rosa sniffled. She hated her allergy. The sneezes always came at the worst time.

In the next inning Rosa was up first.

"Ah choo!" she sneezed, stepping up to the plate.

"Ah choo! Ah choo!" went Zack, making fun.

Just as the first pitch was thrown, Rosa

sneezed. *"Ah choo!"* she said as the ball whizzed by.

"Strike one!" yelled the umpire.

"Sneezy's going to strike out!" yelled Angie.

And it looked like she might. When the next pitch came by Rosa sneezed again. And missed the ball.

"Strike two!" cried the umpire.

"You mean sneeze two!" said Zack, laughing.

Rosa gritted her teeth. She tried hard not to sneeze, but it wasn't easy. As the ball was coming her way she went, *"Ah . . . ah . . . ah . . . ah . . . choo!"* Rosa swung and sneezed at the same time.

Wham! The bat caught the ball and sent it flying. It shot by first like a rocket. Rosa ran all the way to second base.

"Wow!" yelled Henry. "That ball was jet-propelled!"

"Not jet-propelled, sneeze-propelled," said Rosa. She smiled and shouted to Zack. "Calling me Sneezy wasn't very smart, was it?"

"What do you mean?" said Zack.

"You helped me get a hit. You made me so mad I tried extra hard," said Rosa.

"If she's Sneezy then I guess that makes you Dopey," said Henry.

Everyone laughed. Everyone but Zack. "Come on," he growled. "Let's play ball."

Rosa wasn't the last Monster to get a hit. Ginger and Henry got hits too. And when the inning was over the Monsters led, two to one.

"Good work," said Henry. "Keep it up. Maybe we can win this game after all."

For a while it looked as if the Monsters might hold on. But then, in the last inning, the Sharks got three straight hits and loaded the bases.

Zack came up to bat. If he got a hit the Sharks would surely win. If he made an out, the Monsters would win.

"Strike him out!" called Rosa the zombie.

"Shut up, you slimeball!" Zack yelled back.

Ginger pitched the ball.

Zack swung and missed. "Strike one!"

"Good pitch!" cried Jody. She was a skeleton.

"Clam up, you bag of bones!" shouted Zack.

Ginger pitched again. Zack swung and missed again. Strike two!

"One more and he's out!" yelled the werewolf, Darlene.

"Button up, dog breath!" yelled Zack. He snarled and waited for the last pitch.

Ginger wound up. She let the ball fly.

Zack swung.

Whack! The ball came off his bat like a bullet.

"Catch it!" yelled the crowd.

But the Monsters didn't think it would be caught. That's because it was heading right for Melvin. At any moment they expected him to yell "Yikes!" and start running. Then the ball would go into the field. Three runs would score. And the Sharks would go on to win the game.

"Oh, no," thought Melvin as soon as he saw the ball speeding his way. "I've got to get out of here."

But then he thought of something else. He thought of his friend. His very best friend, Flip.

"I can't run away," he thought. He gritted his teeth. "I can't!"

Melvin held out his glove. He shut his eyes.

Pow! The ball slammed into the mitt.

When Melvin opened his eyes, there was the ball. In his glove!

"I caught it!" he shouted.

"Zack, you're out!" cried Henry.

"The game is over!" yelled Ginger.

Rosa ran over and threw her slimy arms around Melvin.

"We won!" she screamed. "You did it! You did it!"

All over the field Monsters started hugging each other. The crowd poured onto the field.

"Flip!" yelled Melvin. "Where are you?"

From somewhere came a bark. Then another.

"Flip!"

The little dog came zooming through the crowd. He skidded to a halt at Melvin's feet. Then he turned a flip and jumped into his best friend's arms.

"My puppy!" cried Melvin, tears running down his cheeks. "Now we'll always be together."

Zack dropped his bat. "I can't believe it," he muttered, over and over. "I just can't believe it."

"I can believe it," said Henry. He slapped Zack on the back. "Tell the Sharks to come by tomorrow. You can start fixing up our clubhouse then."

Zack grunted in reply. Then he turned and walked out of the park. The other Sharks left too, their heads bowed.

The big crowd wanted more. They loved the Monster All-Stars.

"When will you play again?" everyone asked.

"In an hour," said Henry.

"An hour!" exclaimed a bald man. "Where?"

"In Rosa Dorado's garage," said Henry. "Haven't you heard? We're putting on a play, *Return of the Vampire*."

So many people came to Rosa's that the Creepy Creature Club had to put on the show three times.

And when Melvin, the monster from Mars, saved the day at the end of the play everyone cheered. Just like they had at the game.

"Aw, it was nothing," said Melvin, bowing.

"Hooray for Melvin," cried Rosa. "Melvin's our hero."

"Melvin, that was a great catch you made," said Henry. "The greatest catch of the game."

Rosa raised an eyebrow. "Why, Henry, what a nice thing to say. I've never heard you brag about anyone but yourself."

"Aw, it was nothing," said Henry.

"I like you when you're not bragging," said Rosa. "I really do."

"You like me?" said Henry. He smoothed down his hair. "Really?"

"Really," said Rosa. "When you're not bragging you're very nice."

Henry beamed. Rosa liked him! She really did.

Suddenly he felt like the happiest monster on the block. Maybe the happiest in the whole world.

He wanted to shout out the news. But he didn't. For once he kept his mouth shut.

He didn't dare brag. Not about anything.

Even if it was about Rosa, his new best friend.

Monster Jokes

This is Henry Potter again. I don't mean to brag, but I'm the world's funniest comedian. No kidding. Here are some of my favorite monster jokes.

What kind of friends does a zombie have?
Any kind he can dig up.

What did one casket say to the other casket?
Is that you coffin?

Why couldn't the mummy come to the phone?
He was all tied up.

What kind of jewelry do witches like best?
Charm bracelets.

What job did the vampire have on the baseball team?
Bat boy.

Where would you find a cemetery?
On a dead end street.

What is Dracula's favorite building?
The Vampire State building.

What do you get when a cow sees a ghost?
A milk shake.

What does Dracula use to keep his teeth from falling out?
Toothpaste.

What do you call a skeleton who won't work?
Lazybones.

Nurse: There's an invisible man out here with a toothache.
Dentist: Tell him I can't see him.